Two in a Tent

by Molly Brett

© The Medici Society Ltd., London 1969 Printed in England. Code 85503003 8.

2

It *must* be dull living in the country, thought Susan when she came to stay for a weekend with her cousin David, for there were no cinemas, no traffic roaring along, no television, no supermarket, and few shops in the little village, so unlike her home in a big town.

But David was very excited because his mother had promised they should sleep in his tent in the orchard, cook their own meals, and explore the nearby wood and fields all by themselves.

The top windows of the house looked down on the little tent, but the rest of it was screened by the apple trees, and, as they started to arrange their camp, Susan began to think it might be fun in the country after all.

"It's like being in a living picture book!" she exclaimed, looking up into the blue sky where a lark sang, while bright butterflies danced to the hum of bees, laden with golden pollen dust from many flowers, and carried in little baskets on their legs, and a tiny wren perched on a scented spray of honeysuckle trilled a very loud song for so small a bird.

"Quite right, Susan," said David's daddy who had been helping to put up the tent, "nature is always making pictures and telling stories for those who look and listen, and every day is another page with something wonderful to be found in it."

3

"Well, we'd better begin by finding some firewood," suggested David, starting across the stepping stones of the stream which bordered the orchard.

There were plenty of sticks in the wood beyond.

"Oooh! a baby crocodile!" cried Susan, as a little lizard ran over her sandal.

"Look! there's a fox," whispered David as the setting sun caught its bright fur. Then the white tip of his bushy tail disappeared in the bracken and the fox slipped away to his earth, where the vixen and cubs were hoping he would bring back a rabbit for supper.

As they returned the children heard a tapping among the trees, and saw a great spotted woodpecker hunting for insects on a dead branch.

Back in camp a fire was soon blazing and during supper moths fluttered out of the hedge towards the firelight, privet hawk, drinker, currant moth, lime hawk, and a lovely garden tiger moth which had begun life as a woolly bear caterpillar.

"Now we are going on a midnight march," said David raking out the last embers of the fire.

"It isn't midnight but it's getting awfully dark," Susan replied doubtfully, "and—whatever is *that*?" she exclaimed, as a loud 'Tu Whit, Tu Whoo!' came from above.

4

"It's only an owl," explained David, as it passed over on silent wings hunting for mice, and then disappeared into the darkness, while the children watched a tiny pigmy shrew mouse, the smallest British mammal, hide under an ivy-leaf until the danger was past.

Following a path round the wood they heard the queer 'churring' cry of a nightjar, while tawny and barn owls called among the trees, then—something dark fluttered out and Susan clung to David yelling "Oooh! a bat!"

But her cousin laughed at her. "It won't hurt us," he said, "why be scared of a fluffy little mouse with leathery wings instead of feather ones."

"It's called a Flittermouse as it flies about catching the gnats that bite us."

So Susan felt it was silly to be afraid of such a harmless little animal who would sleep through the day hanging upside down in a hollow tree or barn.

They had now come to a leafy hollow with a big hole in the bank. Hart's tongue ferns, with seeds stuck on the backs of the leaves, grew round it.

Susan felt rather scared—perhaps a goblin lived there.

But David knew better as he had been here with his father, and pulled her down under some nut bushes, where they kept so still that a fat little dormouse ran along a branch of briar rose quite close to them.

Presently something moved in the dark entrance to a big hole and a white face with two black stripes appeared, then out came a big grey animal with a brown waistcoat, followed by his mate and two little ones.

"Badgers," whispered David, as the babies romped round their parents.

The badger family ambled away to look for grubs, roots and insects. Before daylight they would return to their home which is called a Sett, and is always kept clean with fresh beds of dry grass or bracken.

It was quite dark when the children returned to their tent and little lights were shining among the grasses.

"Then there *are* fairies in the country!" whispered Susan excitedly.

"No, *worms*—glow worms!" laughed David, catching one, and Susan saw it was really a little beetle in a striped coat. The gentleman glow worm had wings but no light like his lady, who was unable to fly.

David's mother came down from the house to say it was time for bed, and soon the children were wriggling into their sleeping bags.

Suddenly David jumped up with a yell, for a hedgehog had curled up in a prickly ball just where he lay, having wandered into the tent while looking for slugs and beetles for supper.

Susan offered a saucer of milk and the visitor soon uncurled, lapped it up, then scuttled away making a snuffy gruffy sort of noise as a 'thank you.'

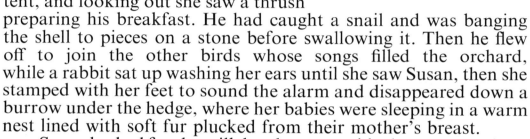

Soon the children were fast asleep, while from a hawthorn bush came the lovely song of a nightingale, the slim brown bird who sings in the dark.

Susan was awakened very early next morning by a tapping outside the tent, and looking out she saw a thrush preparing his breakfast. He had caught a snail and was banging the shell to pieces on a stone before swallowing it. Then he flew off to join the other birds whose songs filled the orchard, while a rabbit sat up washing her ears until she saw Susan, then she stamped with her feet to sound the alarm and disappeared down a burrow under the hedge, where her babies were sleeping in a warm nest lined with soft fur plucked from their mother's breast.

Susan looked for the milk bottle put outside the tent overnight, and found a bluetit pecking a hole in the top to get the cream inside. On seeing her he flew away to join other members of his big family, the great tits, coal tits, and long tailed tits.

After breakfast the children ran up to the house to collect the lunch David's mother had packed for them.

"Daddy and I are driving to see a friend in hospital" she said, "I will leave the house key at the farm down the road."

"We like our tent better than the house," replied David and Susan and, saying 'good-bye', they set off to see the harvester at work in the big cornfield.

At the stream a deer was drinking but started away when she saw the children.

"Look! there's a baby," cried Susan in delight gazing after the pretty spotted little thing.

"That's a fawn," David told her, "it may be only a few hours old but it can run about already, not pushed around in a pram for months like a human baby."

As they crossed the stepping stones a fat brown water rat or vole splashed into the water and a heron flew overhead, while an otter disappeared downstream. His webbed paws and strong tail like a rudder make him a wonderful underwater swimmer as he hunts fish.

His home or holt is under the roots of an old willow tree bending low over the stream.

"Are those *chickens* swimming?" enquired Susan pointing to some small black birds paddling along, and jerking their heads as if by clockwork.

But her cousin said they were moorhens with a little red cap on their beaks, while the coots in sober black had a white patch.

After scrambling up the bank fringed with water forget-me-nots and purple loosestrife they came to a big pine tree and a cone hit David on the nose. It was half eaten and other pieces lay scattered on the ground.

"That means there's a squirrel about," said he, and looking up they saw it scrambling down behind a tree trunk. Then it scratched among the dead leaves and found a nut hidden in the autumn, when the clever squirrels collect a store of food for the winter.

"Is that its nest?" asked Susan, pointing to a big bundle of sticks and twigs, so David climbed the tree to see.

As he did so a woodpigeon flew out, while a jay squawked in alarm, flapping wings barred with blue.

But it was not a squirrel's home or drey; instead two big black and white birds with long tails fluttered round with chuckling cries.

It was a magpie's nest and when David had climbed down again he put his hand in his pocket and brought out—some milk bottle tops, a pebble, two glass beads, and a teaspoon.

Magpies love things that glitter so these had been collected and hidden in the nest.

They could now hear the clatter of the combine harvester at work, but on reaching the edge of the field David suddenly pulled Susan back and, looking down she saw a tiny leveret, or baby hare, lying in a shallow form of grass just by her feet.

Unlike a blind and naked young rabbit it had been born with a fur coat and open eyes, able to run about or lie quietly in this grassy bed, waiting for mother to come and feed it.

Next Susan found a harvest mouse's nest fixed on three corn stalks, among scarlet poppies, and chicory, whose lovely blue flowers die in a day. It was beautifully made of grasses woven into a ball. There was no door but presently a tiny nose pushed through the side of the loosely woven nest, and the little mouse climbed nimbly down a cornstalk. She would have to find a new home for the winter safe underground, as the harvester went round the field and the corn fell like a golden wave.

Cock sparrows wearing little black bibs, and a pair of beautiful goldfinches flew off, followed by a cock pheasant with a long tail.

"Look, baby strawberries!" said Susan pointing to some wild ones among the clover and yellow toadflax.

"Just right for lunch," replied David, "But watch the corn moving over there, something is coming out.

Presently a slim ginger brown weasel appeared carrying a tiny baby in her mouth. After hiding it in a tangle of fragrant bindweed she returned with two more, determined to save them from the great harvester dragon.

High above a hawk hovered, spread wings still, then dropped like a stone, but the weasel had vanished.

"She's a fierce little creature but very brave," said David as they ate their lunch, and watched bumble bees, grasshoppers, ants, and a ladybird among the grasses.

"These little red flowers are all closing up," said Susan, pointing to a Scarlet Pimpernel beside her.

"That means it is going to rain so we had better get back," replied David, jumping up as dark clouds shadowed the sunshine and there was a distant rumble of thunder.

The children ran all the way to the tent as rain began to patter down, lightning flashed, and the thunder grew louder.

"Too wet to get the house key from the farm," panted David, "we'll be alright here until the storm is over."

He thought it a fine adventure, but Susan didn't like thunder storms, and wished she was safe indoors.

Suddenly something blundered against the tent, Susan squealed, but David looked out and saw the little fawn they had seen by the stream.

It was so wet and bewildered that it allowed him to bring it into the tent, and lay quietly while Susan dried it with a towel, and quite forgot to be frightened of the thunder as she comforted the baby animal.

The storm went on for a long time and it began to get dark.

"Daddy will have to come and rescue us with his big umbrella," said David, trying to sound braver than he felt. His parents should have returned by now.

But Mummy and Daddy were still miles away in the car, for the road was flooded and they had to drive a long way round to get home.

At last the rain seemed to be stopping, the thunder died down and the children looked out of the tent.

Peering into the twilight they saw something very strange indeed—the ground all round their little tent was MOVING!

There was *water* rippling and running everywhere for the stream, swollen by the rain, had flooded the orchard.

David and Susan started to splash through it, but the ground was uneven and in a moment Susan had stumbled into a hollow where the water was quite deep.

David pulled her up, crying and dripping, and looked round in vain for a way to dry land, for the water was still rising and it was almost dark.

Just then the little fawn followed them out of the tent and paddled past. This gave David an idea and hand in hand the children followed him.

The fawn seemed to sense where the water was shallow and soon led them through it to higher ground, where he disappeared into the wood, while David and Susan ran through the trees, on to the road, and in at the front gate just as David's parents drove up in the car.

After hot baths and supper they all agreed it had been a real adventure with a happy ending, thanks to the little fawn.

Before Susan went home next day she picked a big bunch of wild flowers for her mother who was an artist, and painted a picture of them for Susan's bedroom, and told her the names of each one, so she won't forget camping in the country and all the exciting things to be seen there.